THE
CROSSING

MICHAEL CONNELLY
THE CROSSING

First published in Great Britain in 2015 by Orion Books,
an imprint of The Orion Publishing Group Ltd
Carmelite House, 50 Victoria Embankment
London EC4Y 0DZ

An Hachette UK Company

3 5 7 9 10 8 6 4

A CIP catalogue record for this book is
available from the British Library.

ISBN (Hardback) 978 1 4091 4552 3
ISBN (Export Trade Paperback) 978 1 4091 4590 5
ISBN (Ebook) 978 1 4091 4589 9

Printed in Great Britain by Clays Ltd, St Ives plc

The Orion Publishing Group's policy is to use papers that
are natural, renewable and recyclable products and made
from wood grown in sustainable forests. The logging and
manufacturing processes are expected to conform to the
environmental regulations of the country of origin.

www.orionbooks.co.uk

In memory of Simon Christenson

THE
CROSSING

APRIL FOOLS' DAY

Ellis and Long were four car lengths behind the motorcycle on Ventura Boulevard. They were eastbound, coming up to the big curve where the road would turn south and head down through the pass into Hollywood.

Ellis was behind the wheel, where he preferred to be, even though he was the senior partner and could dictate to Long who drove and who rode shotgun. Long was looking down at the screen on his phone, staring at the video feed, watching over what they called their investments.

The car felt good. It felt strong. There was little play in the wheel. Ellis felt solidly in control. He saw an opening in the right lane and pushed his foot down. The car jumped forward.

Long looked up.

"What are you doing?"

"Getting rid of a problem."

"What?"

"Before it's a problem."

He had caught up and was now riding next to the motorcycle. He glanced over and saw the rider's black boots and the orange flames painted on the gas tank. The flames matched the color of the Camaro.

He pulled a few feet ahead and as the road curved right he allowed the car to drift into the left lane, following the laws of centrifugal force.

He heard the rider yell. He kicked at the side of the car and then gunned it to try to move ahead. That was his mistake. He should have braked and bailed but he tried to gun his way out of it. Ellis was ready for the move and pinned the accelerator. The Camaro surged into the left lane, completing the cutoff.

Ellis heard brakes squeal and a long sustained blast of a car horn as the motorcycle went into the oncoming traffic lanes. Then he heard the high-pitched scraping of steel and the inevitable impact of metal against metal.

Ellis smiled and kept going.

ACKNOWLEDGMENTS

My special thanks to my editor Djinn von Noorden who was midwife to this novel. Without her expert skills and endless patience it might well have been stillborn. To Antony Farrell and The Lilliput Press for their faith. To my countless friends who read early drafts but especially to those from my Creative Writing MPhil class in Trinity, Jean Flltcroft, Patricia Wallace and Christina Dowling. To my dear friends Ruth and Steven Williams for believing in this. To my cousin Frances for filling in the missing pieces from her extraordinary knowledge of family history and driving me to Wissant where it all made sense. To Punch for all of his lifetime support, correcting the flying scenes, donating a bomb trailer (found in the yard at home) to the Lincolnshire Heritage Aviation Centre in Tony's memory and for, as he has always done, keeping the home fires burning while I chased my dreams. And finally to my darling mother for so much and especially for the story.

flak and exploded on impact at about 6 pm. A few words ended the story and recorded the end of nine short lives.

Because the area was still held by the Germans it was some hours before the resistance could visit the site and some days before the remains could be moved. One can imagine the chaos that ensued in the immediate aftermath of the German retreat.

On 2 October the good people of Wissant buried the crew in their own cemetery behind the village. They took the trouble to have a priest bless them. There were three coffins but such was the effect of the explosion only two were filled. The grave is considered to be a collective one, which is as it should be. Only one dog tag was ever found, and it did not belong to Tony.

Four pilots are commemorated on the engine nacelles of the famous Avro Lancaster S for Sugar in the RAF Museum in Hendon. One of them is Pilot Officer A.B.L. Tottenham – Tony. His brother Nick Tottenham devoted his life to the welfare of war veterans through his work with the Returned Servicemen's League in Australia. He was awarded Life Membership of the League in 1992, which is described as 'a single honour of great importance'.

'*Non, mais ...*' He gropes around on his cluttered desk. 'Last week I received something. Ah, here it is.' He fishes two photocopied pages from the brown envelope in his hand. 'Someone send this here, I don't know.' He places the pages on the desk in front of us. There, from the middle of the top page, is Tony's impossibly young face smiling back at us, so like those of our mothers. It is captioned *Wissant LM587* and under the photograph *Le pilote Tottenham*.

'But that's him,' we cry in unison and then we can hardly speak. We turn to the second page and there is a photograph of a Canadian soldier going through the debris of LM587. We are looking at what was left of the last Lancaster flown by Tony. The wreckage appears to be on the top of the cliff. Behind it is a battery of the Atlantic wall, its gun facing towards us.

'Where is this place?' Frances asks.

'Floringzelle,' the curator says, waving his hand through the window towards the lighthouse at Gris Nez. He points back to the picture.

'This is the *Grosser Kurfürst*, which was there right on the Cap, *là-bas*. That Lancaster, it crashed just there,' he said.

The pages had been sent to the museum only a few days before our visit by Phillippe Goldstein and were an extract from a scholarly book written by a local historian called Hugues Chevalier, entitled *Les combats de la Libération du Pas-de-Calais*. M. Goldstein sent them to the museum, on the off-chance that, on the seventieth anniversary, some family belonging to the crew of this doomed Lancaster might make the very journey that Frances and I were now making.

From the two pages we learn more: the author quoted a report compiled in 1947 by Raphael Goldstein, our opportunistic correspondent's father, for the Missing Research & Enquiry Service. The elder M. Goldstein had interviewed the former members of the Resistance who still lived in Wissant at that time. According to them, the Lancaster came in low over Cap Gris Nez, was hit by